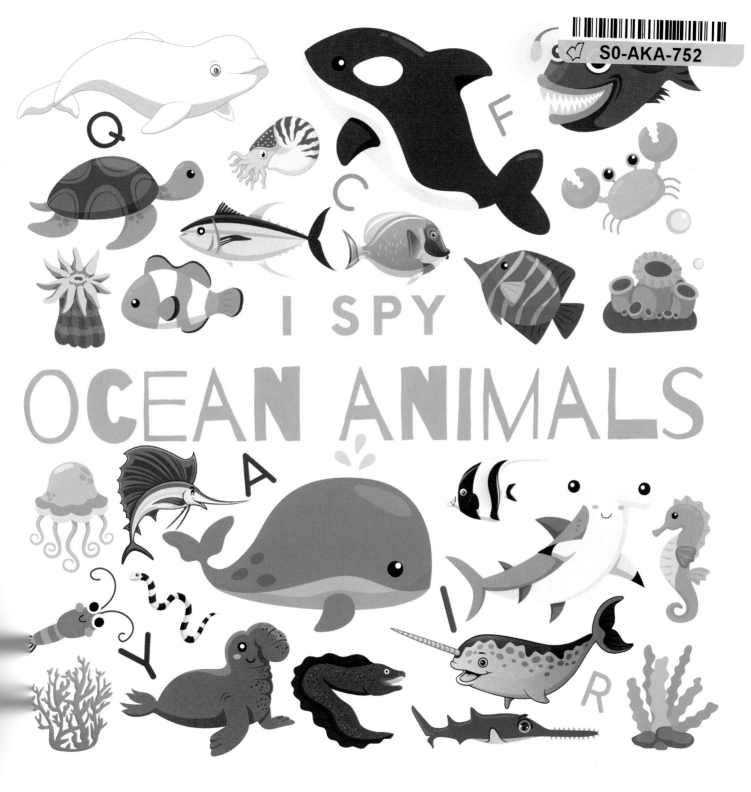

I SPY

OCEAN ANIMALS

S0-AKA-752

I Spy Ocean Animals
Copyright 2020 © Alek Malkovich
All rights reserved.

No part of this book may be reproduce or used
in any form without the written consent of the
author and publisher.

ISBN: 9798645688028

Printed in the USA

I SPY with my little eyes, something beginning with...

A

A is for

Anglerfish

I SPY with my little eyes, something beginning with...

B

B is for

Beluga

I SPY with my little eyes, something beginning with...

C and D

C is for

Clownfish

D is for

Dolphin

I SPY with my little eyes, something beginning with...

E is for

Eel

I SPY with my little eyes, something beginning with...

F

is for

Flounder

I SPY with my little eyes, something beginning with...

G and H

G is for

Grouper

H is for

Hammerhead shark

I SPY with my little eyes, something beginning with...

I is for

Isopod

I SPY with my little eyes, something beginning with...

J is for

Jellyfish

I SPY with my little eyes, something beginning with...

K and L

K is for
Killerwhale

L is for
Lionfish

I SPY with my little eyes, something beginning with...

M

M is for

Marlin

I SPY with my little eyes, something beginning with...

N is for

Narwhal

I SPY with my little eyes, something beginning with...

O and P

O is for

Oyster

P is for

Puffer

I SPY with my little eyes, something beginning with...

Q is for

Quohog

I SPY with my little eyes, something beginning with...

R is for

Ray

I SPY with my little eyes, something beginning with...

S is for
Seahorse

T is for
Turtle

I SPY with my little eyes, something beginning with...

U is for

Unicorn fish

I SPY with my little eyes, something beginning with...

V is for

Vampire squid

I SPY with my little eyes, something beginning with...

W and X

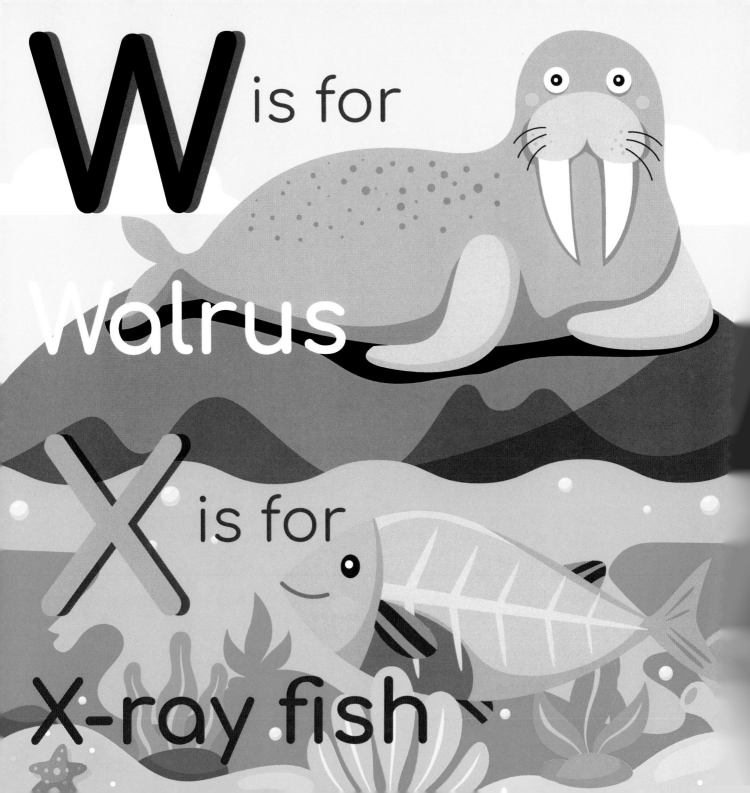

W is for

Walrus

X is for

X-ray fish

I SPY with my little eyes, something beginning with...

Y is for

Yellowfin tuna

I SPY with my little eyes, something beginning with...

Z is for

Zooplankton